little miss Splendid

by Roger Hargreaves

© Mrs Roger Hargreaves 1981
Printed and published 1991 under licence from Price Stern Sloan Inc.,
Los Angeles. All rights reserved.
Published in Great Britain by World International Publishing Limited,
An Egmont Company, Egmont House, P.O. Box 111, Great Ducie Street,
. Manchester M60 3BL. Printed in Finland. ISBN 0-7408-0486-6
Reprinted 1993
A CIP catalogue record for this book is available from the British Library

Nothing was too good for little Miss Splendid.

She lived in a huge house surrounded by large gardens.

She slept in an enormous bed with silk sheets and silk pillowcases.

She bathed in a gold bath.

And she dined off silver plates.

Oh, she was splendid!

At least, she thought so.

Little Miss Splendid thought a lot of herself.

In fact, she thought about little else!

One day, while taking a stroll around her gardens, little Miss Splendid came upon a small door in one of the walls.

She'd never noticed it before.

"I wonder what's through here?" she thought and, opening the door, she stepped through.

She found herself on a road.

Along came Mr Small, out for a short walk.

"Good morning," he remarked politely, raising his hat.

Little Miss Splendid stuck her nose even higher in the air, and walked past him as if he wasn't there.

"What a common little man," she thought to herself.

She came to a bus stop.

Mr Happy and Mr Daydream were waiting for a bus into town.

"Hello," grinned Mr Happy.

"Who are you?"

"I," she replied, "am Splendid!"

"Oh," said Mr Happy.

"Are you going to catch the bus?" asked Mr Daydream.

"Me?" she said.

"The bus?"

"Never!!"

"I," she went on, "have never ever in the whole of my life travelled on a bus!"

An expression of distaste crossed her face.

"You have to sit next to people on buses," she went on. "And that would never do!"

"Oh" said Mr Happy, and scratched his head.

He couldn't think of anything to say.

Miss Splendid walked off with her nose very high in the air.

Miss Splendid arrived in town.

She looked at herself in all the shop windows as she walked down the street.

"I must say," she thought to herself, "I do look absolutely splendid."

And then something caught her eye.

There, in the middle of the window of the hat shop, was a hat.

Not just a hat.

A hat and a half!

The most magnificent, sumptuous, desirable, gorgeous, spectacular, amazing, splendid hat you've ever seen.

Miss Splendid marched into the shop.

She snapped her fingers, and a saleslady hurried to her side.

"Good morning Madam," the saleslady said.

Miss Splendid ignored her.

"Can I help you?"

"I," announced Miss Splendid, "wish to try on the hat in the window!"

Miss Splendid looked at herself in the mirror.

"Magnificent," she breathed.

"I look absolutely magnificent!"

"I'll take it," she announced.

"But don't you want to know how much it costs?" asked the saleslady.

"Costs?" queried Miss Splendid loftily.

"I never discuss money matters!"

"Send me the bill!"

And she marched out of the shop.

Little Miss Splendid stood on the pavement,
and held up her hand.

"Taxi!" she announced in a loud important
voice.

A taxi stopped.

"Take me home," she ordered, and went to get
in, but of course she couldn't.

Her new hat was much too large to fit through
the taxi door.

"Driver," she said. "You should purchase
yourself a larger taxi!"

"In the meantime," she went on, "I shall walk!"

The taxi driver grinned.

Little Miss Splendid walked along.

"Perhaps it's better to walk," she thought to herself.

"So that everyone has the chance to admire my magnificent new hat."

But then it happened.

It started to rain!

And the trouble was, the more it started to rain, the more it rained.

And the trouble was, the more it rained, the more Miss Splendid got wet.

And the trouble was, the wetter she got, the wetter her hat got.

What a sorry sight!

Don't you agree?

The bus, on its return journey from town, passed her.

Mr Happy and Mr Daydream, on their way home and sitting in the dry, looked out of the window.

"I say," remarked Mr Happy, looking out at the bedraggled figure trudging along in the wet. "What a splendid sight!"

Mr Daydream giggled.

"Splendid," he agreed.

Miss Splendid, looking anything but splendid, arrived home.

However, after a hot bath in her gold bath, and after a boiled egg in a gold egg cup, eaten with a silver spoon, she felt much better.

In fact, later on, she spent an extremely pleasant evening looking at...

Well.

What do you think she spent all evening looking at?

No!

Not television.

Herself!

In the mirror!